FRANCINE BASSÈDE

Francine Bassède was born in Nîmes, in the South of France.
She holds degrees in law and political science and she has studied fine art
in Aix-en-Provence and Montpellier. Her parents were rural doctors
in France, and Ms Bassède developed as a child a deep love for the nature
of Provence. She now lives in Montpellier with her husband, their three
children and their many animals.

Also by Francine Bassède from Siphano Picture Books:

GEORGE IS PAINTING HIS HOUSE
COOKING WITH GEORGE
A DAY WITH THE BELLYFLOPS

ISBN 1-903078-05-9

© Siphano Picture Books, 1997 for the text and illustrations
UK edition text by Charles Bloom and Dominic Barth

First UK edition by Siphano Picture Books, 1999

This paperback edition is published in Great Britain in 2000 by Siphano Picture Books Ltd.,
P.O. Box 2621, Castle Cary, Somerset BA7 7YJ

Printed in Italy by Grafiche AZ, Verona

FRANCINE BASSEDE

GEORGE'S STORE
on the seashore

SIPHANO PICTURE BOOKS

Every summer morning,
George wakes up early to set
up his store at the shore.
His good friend Mary is always
there to help.

First, one beach
umbrella. Mary
props it against
the door of the shop.

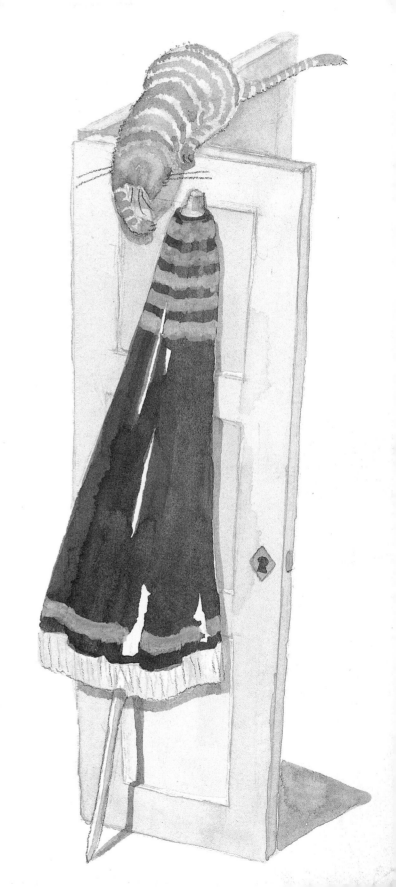

Next, two fishing nets,
for catching little fish,
crabs and sea urchins.

One, two...
One, two...
One, two, three ducky floaty
things: green, blue, and red!

Four beach balls. Mary
arranges them on the floor
of the store.

"Be careful Mary, watch
your claws," George warns.

Next, five striped
shirts of cotton,
soft and cool.

Six pails. Mary arranges them on the top shelf.

A hat is indispensable
at the beach. Mary hangs
seven for the shop.

Eight shovels...
For making deep holes
and tall sand castles.

Freshly squeezed orange juice!
Very tasty in the fresh sea air;
there are nine glasses.

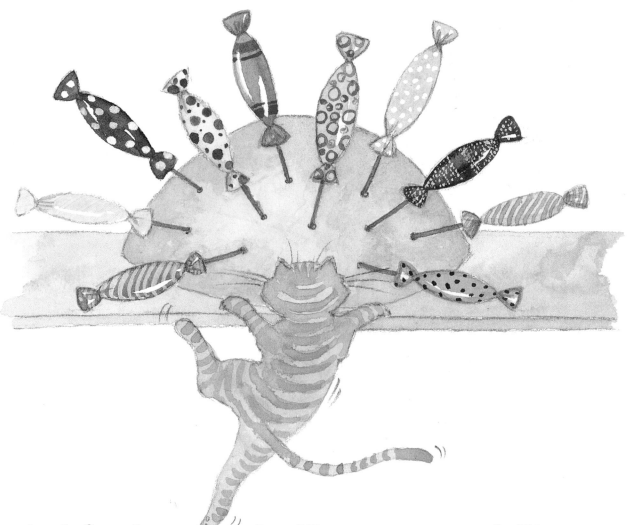

And for those who like sweets, ten lollipops in ten wonderful flavours: strawberry, lemon, mint, chocolate and caramel, licorice, honey, apricot, raspberry and black currant.

A fine assortment.

George and Mary have
set up everything.
The store is open.
The customers
will be here soon!